The Adventures of Coach And Little Dell

My First Tie

Written by:
Tanae Denean Eskridge &
Brandon M. Frame

Copyright © 2018 by
Tanae Denean Eskridge & Brandon M. Frame

All rights reserved.
No part of this publication may be reproduced or transmitted
by any means, without prior permission of the publisher.

ISBN: 978-1-78324-109-5

Published by Wordzworth
www.wordzworth.com

A book series with stories that make kids smile, laugh, and learn. Thoughtful books that celebrate the multicultural society we live in.

Author's Mission

We celebrate diversity and childhood with great stories and lessons. We are also introducing a positive black male character to children's literature. Coach is a fixer, a teacher, a motivator, a mentor, and an all-around great guy.

I am an expert in the art of the 1st grade.

Expert means to know a lot, and I think I almost learned it all.

I learned to fix a tire, Coach showed me on the first day of school.

I joined my first sports team, and I think it's pretty cool.

I can brush my own teeth and wash my own face,

and every day I put on clean underwear and say grace.

I turn my homework packet in on time every week.

I made some super cool new friends, Anton, Omar, and Maleek.

Now, I'm ready for a NEW CHALLENGE.

I love learning things that are new.

Mrs. Stacey said I am INQUISITIVE, and my mom said that's true.

We had two weeks until picture day,

and I already knew what I was going to do...

dress like my dad—he loves the color bLUe.

I waited at the gate just like I always do:

Dave Yun, Tiff Bee, and me...

waiting for my mom to pick up our team of three.

Mom pulled up to the school with a baSKet oF SWeet treatS.

She said you should always show love with good food to eat.

She gave us a sample, the rest were for our Coach to keep.

I couldn't wait to get HOME and pick which tie of my dad's I would wear. He has ONE MILLION ties hanging in his closet next to his underwear.

My dad was SMart just like President Obama.

He said a man should always dress nice
and LOOK HiS Very best.

My mom always says my dad is SMOOTHer than the rest.

We sat at the table: Dad, Mom, my siblings, and me.

Together we always say a prayer of thanks.

Dad asked me if I have any good news, because bad news stinks.

Mom said it's just a few more days until my first picture day.

I was so excited for that day I could have screamed hooray.

I woke up **extra early** the next day just to watch Dad get dressed.

I needed to know exactly what to do; I wanted to put it to the test.

He stood in the closet putting on one pant leg at a time.

He picked out a short sleeved shirt and said it was for the springtime.

Then he looked at me in the mirror, with a very serious face:

"Son, a man must take **pride in his appearance**. It's easier to give respect when you have self-respect."

At that moment, **Magic** happened as he picked out his favorite tie.

He looped it and looped it and looped it up high.

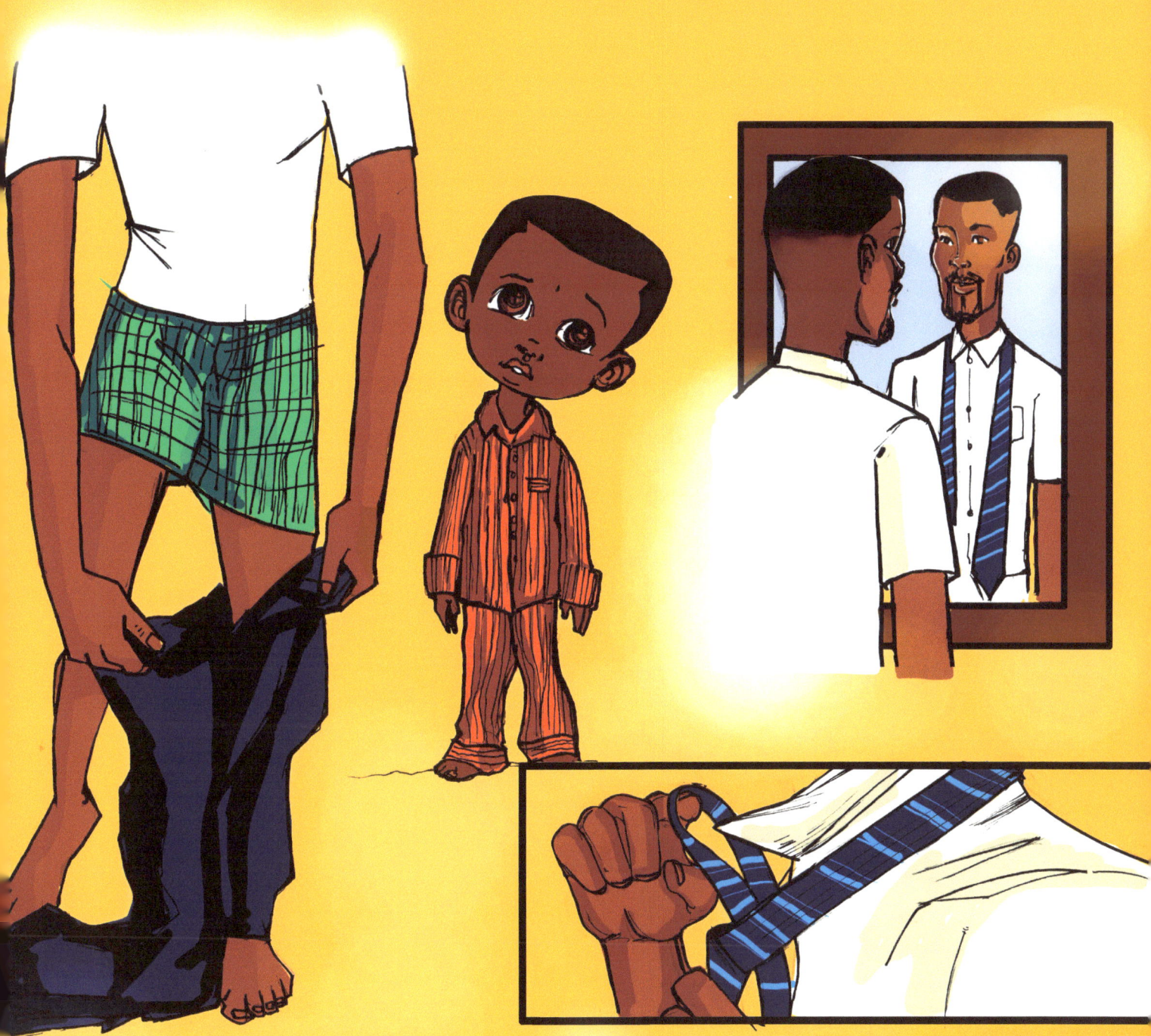

Mom yelled my name, and that meant I needed to get dressed.

I hurried and put on my clothes.

I made sure I looked My very best.

I stopped by Dad's closet to get a tie,

folded it neatly, and then tucked it away.

I couldn't wait to show my friends

how to tie a tie the Loop da Loop Way.

Fellas, you have to see this! It's awesome what I can do.

I pulled out my dad's tie, but I couldn't get the loop da loop through.

I looped it to the left and then I looped it to the right.

I looped it up and looped it down,

but it wouldn't get tight.

Ms. Stacey then said it was time to start our school day.

I was so bummed, I didn't even want to go out for recess to play.

Coach came to talk to me when he noticed I was a little grey.

Low and grey is what my nana calls having a bad day.

"Picture day is coming up, and I'm not ready.

I just feel so sad, and my heart feels so heavy."

"Little Dell, I know you're feeling down.

You can't let a bad moment turn your SMiLe into a frown."

He told me a joke or two,

and before I knew it, my smile grew.

"I think it's time for you to get rid of your grey,

so go run, jump, skip, and play."

I returned to class when I heard

Principal Tiger over the loudspeaker saying,

"Yeeeebeeedeee yeeebeedooo!

This is a FrieNdLy reminder to look your best on picture day.

Please brush your teeth extra long,

and don't be wrinkled that would be so wrong.

Make sure those smiles are bright and true.

Yeeeebeeedeee yeeebeedooo!

My name is Principal Tiger, and it's been great talking to you."

Principle Tiger said we should look our best for picture day,

and I felt like that meant I needed to wear my dad'S Favorite tie.

I really needed to learn the loop da loop way.

Anton, Omar, and Maleek agreed with me.

We all decided to wear bLUe ties and matching bLUe jeans.

The next morning, I decided that NOTHING would get in my way.

I ran down the hall to watch Dad prepare for another work day.

When he started looking for his favorite gray tie–

which was in my bag–I didn't know what to say.

I just walked back to my room and started to prepare for My day.

Dad and Mom wondered where his grey tie might lay.

This day was starting out as another that was low and grey

I JUMPed in the car with Dave Yun and Tiff Bee.

Mom WHiSKed us off to school like she always does us three.

I explained my problem to my friends and asked what I should do.

Omar said I should move to Puerto Rico and change my name to San Dru.

Anton said it wasn't a big deal,

but I should tell my dad because his dad said MeN Keep it real.

Ms. Stacey said, "Class, I hope you're all preparing for picture day."

I look at my dad's tie in my bag.

My Heart was racing, and I felt so bad.

It was the LONGEST day of school ever...

I accidentally stole my dad's tie, and I just wanted to feel better.

During P.E., I didn't even want to run, jump, skip, or play.

Coach asked if I was having another grey day.

I just couldn't keep it in and had to tell the truth.

I started to cry before I even had something to say.

I told him about the part where I was excited for picture day

and how I wanted to dress like my dad

and be just like him in every single way.

I told Coach that I stole my dad's tie and

couldn't make the loop da loop the same way.

I told him I might have to move to Puerto Rico and change my name.

I also told him how a man should always look his best because

no one would respect a man that has no self-respect.

Coach led me aside to give me a plan.

One Little man and one tall man.

He said, "You are human and humans make mistakes."

"When you see your dad, tell him the truth—that's all it takes."

"Honesty is the best way, as we always say.

Be the first to apologize and treat everyone the right way."

I felt much better. Coach always knows what to say and do.

He said a Father-and-Son bond can't be broken

and there's nothing more true.

As soon as I got home, I ran into my dad's office and told him the truth.

He said, "Son, taking anything without asking is wrong.
Respect is not given, it's earned.

You earned my respect by telling me the truth.

I am your father and anything that

belongs to me belongs to you, too."

"Son, your grandpa taught me the LOOP da LOOP way. I'll give you a lesson, but it's your job to practice every day."

The next few days came and went, and it was FiNaLLy picture day.

I was amazed at how fancy everyone looked in every which way.

Tiff Bee wore her PurPLe, fluffy Easter dress

with PiNK and white ruffled socks and heels, no less!

Dave Yun had on a greeN striped suit with greeN shiny shoes.

ANTON, OMAR, MALEEK,

and I wore jeans, shirts and ties in all BLUES.

Mom said we looked like a 90'S SINGING GROUP.

Dad said we OUT-DRESSED THE REST, our little troupe.

Coach had on basketball shorts with his favorite white tee,
but he said he wore a blue tie just for me.
Principal Tiger was clearly dressed the best.
She had on a red, green, and black dress.
Her nails were royal blue and her jewelry was extra shiny, too...
picture day was a really exciting thing to do.

We sat for our PHotoS and for class pictures, too.
I am now an eXpert at picture day and tying the Loop da Loop.

Mary McLeod Bethune Elementary School 2019

CPSIA information can be obtained
at www.ICGtesting.com
Printed in the USA
BVHW022107290319
544127BV00001B/1/P